Praise for THE GIRL & THE FOX PIRATE

These stories by Kate Gehan are by turns searing, delightful, and heartbreaking. Here, the ordinary soon becomes extraordinary. Beauty is reclaimed. Darkness, triumphantly beaten back (or not!). Gehan's voice is brimming with candor, deft humor, and intelligence. The Girl and the Fox Pirate is a collection by a writer in full command of her craft. Highly recommended.

—KATHY FISH, author of *Together We Can Bury It*

The Girl and the Fox Pirate fills the reader's heart with wonder and pretty, arresting little stories exploring the dreamy, the magical, the mysterious, the unexpected. Kate Gehan is a fantastic, delightful, never-wastes-a-word writer with a knack for punchy, killer endings. This is a charming, keen collection of creatures and treasures where even the darkness crackles and zaps with tiny electric lights.

—LEESA CROSS-SMITH, author of *Every Kiss A War* and *Whiskey & Ribbons*

Kate Gehan crafts deeply emotional, magical tales—talking pigs, mermaids, punk rockers, suburban parents run amok through dreamy landscapes, where she brilliantly catalogs the absurdity of modern life. Gehan's voice is captivating and comical, taming from the wildness of the world folk heroes for a new age. A stunning debut.

—ROBERT JAMES RUSSELL, author of *Mesilla* and *Sea of Trees*

Kate Gehan has written a keenly observed and astute debut. Bravery here manifests itself in unconventional ways, as her characters struggle to cope with grief and want. Gehan's gift is all over these pages; her stories are spare, her insight enormous, making this a heartbreaking and a memorable meditation.

—SARA LIPPMANN, author of *Doll Palace*

More praise for THE GIRL & THE FOX PIRATE

Reminiscent of Jayne Anne Phillips' Black Tickets, the pieces in Kate Gehan's The Girl and the Fox Pirate are stories and poems at the same time – brief, lyrical glimpses into the richest interior worlds. Gehan's sentences are crystals, beautiful and sharp, revealing hidden facets of ordinary people in a uniquely brilliant light. A sparkling debut.

   —JESSICA TREADWAY, author of *Lacy Eye* and *How Will I Know You?*

Story after story, Kate Gehan managed to take me by surprise. In just a few pages, or even a paragraph, she dazzles with words, capturing a lifetime of love and longing and the occasional dragon. Gehan's collection The Girl and The Fox Pirate is a charmer and a delight.

   —MARCY DERMANSKY, author of *The Red Car*

Kate Gehan's debut is a touching, provocative take on domestic dreams and nightmares. This is a world of beautiful babies, magical beasts, promising futures, beauty faded, and opportunities missed. Gehan is a master. What wonderfully cock-eyed and crafted tales! The Girl and The Fox Pirate is a treasure trove to explore over and over again.

   —ALICE KALTMAN, author of *Staggerwing*

In The Girl and the Fox Pirate, Kate Gehan presents an illuminating look into how the fantastic can seamlessly operate inside the domestic sphere. The stories in this collection propel headlong into fabulous, jewel-studded worlds, yet maintain a definitive sense of place. Startling in its beauty, Gehan's work is profoundly dynamic, and marks her as an important new voice in fiction.

   — KRISTEN N. ARNETT, author of *Felt in the Jaw*

The Girl & The Fox Pirate

The Girl & The Fox Pirate

Stories by
Kate Gehan

MOJAVE RIVER PRESS
APPLE VALLEY, CALIFORNIA

My first thanks must go to Michael Dwayne Smith, who believed in my stories and nurtured the best in my writing, offering his poetic gifts and time to make this book possible. I appreciate his partnership on the publishing journey with Mojave River Press. Thanks to all the editors who published my work and gave me wings, and to my generous friends and readers. Leesa Cross-Smith has used her voice to lift me in the most meaningful way and I am unendingly grateful for the glow of her creative spirit. Early on, Barbara Starsky and Dennis Lord taught me the discipline of writing. Elaine Benson and Michael Yellin gave me reason to keep going. Ben Brooks, Jessica Treadway, Sam Baber, and Jeremiah Hakunky helped me to find my voice, and Kathy Fish's guidance strengthens it. Special thanks to Craig Dorfman, Georgia Bellas, Amanda Miska, Ashely Strosnider, and Lori Sambol Brody, whose support along the way sustained me. I very much love my first readers, Sally Ann Rhea and Jane Rhea Vernier, my parents, Helen and Bill Gretz, and my brothers Will and Karl. I am thankful to Dave for giving me some space to write. Finally, and most of all, the crazy adoration I have for my boys is a blessed magic.

Book design by Michael Dwayne Smith

MOJAVE RIVER PRESS
Apple Valley, California
MojaveRiverPress.com
All rights reserved

ISBN: 978-1-63120-008-3

For my grandmothers, Judy and Janis.

CONTENTS

Now They Would Behave

THE DRAGON was loose again.

"Did it slip past when you went out for the paper this morning?" Darcy began.

"I just woke up!" Maurice closed his eyes for a long moment to smother his agitation. He wasn't even wearing pants.

From time to time, the dragon escaped because it was desperate to fly free. "It's regenerating energy," Darcy worried.

She stuck her head out the window to review the damage. Pockmarks shadowed the back gate where the dragon licked the wood with its studded tongue. Smoke lines ran up the house siding, marking the creature's path to flight.

"Lewis! Did you see it fly over the fence? What do I tell you?"

"Always stake the dragon." Lewis used the singsong voice his mother disliked. He thought he had locked it down overnight. "It's not my fault."

The family had plans to go to the art museum's special mini-golf course, and if they spent any time looking for the dragon, the day would get too hot.

Maurice had overslept, and his mistake fanned rage. "Get ready, Lewis!" he shouted. "I will be ticked if we have to wait in long lines. You're the one so keen on going!"

Maurice did not care for the competitiveness derived from amusements with his wife and son, but family outings were important.

Of course, Darcy was ready to go, dressed in her smart pegged pants and vintage top. She was always prepared, always waiting for the boys. Even the dragon was mostly hers to manage.

Darcy was the one bothered most by its lunging for other dragons—no one else cared about controlling it.

As they left the driveway, she shook her head at the charred roof tiles, which advertised the terrible behavior to the neighbors.

Maurice had landed on a 70s radio station and the sexy, cheesy disco beat made Darcy queasy. "I hate this song!" She punched the button, embarrassed for them all.

There was a line for golf at the museum and the concrete pavilion emanated heat at least ten degrees higher than the air. Lewis whined about his forgotten sunglasses and wanted a pair in the gift shop. Maurice roared, "Twenty dollars for a pair you'll just lose is insane!"

On the course Darcy managed par and even under on a few of the holes, but hit a ball out of bounds, and she was woozy by the tenth hole because it was past lunchtime. Lewis threw his club and cursed after driving his ball into a water hazard. Maurice aggressively stopped keeping score.

At the twelfth hole, difficult and "rigged" according to Lewis, the family discovered the dragon hiding behind a plaster triceratops.

"Stupid dragon!" Maurice muttered, relieved.

"It thought the dinosaur was a dragon!" Lewis laughed.

"It just wants to be with its own kind," said Darcy, as she cautiously approached and chained it down. Now they would behave.

At dusk, Darcy walked through the neighborhood up to the eucalyptus grove at the top of the hill and leaned against a tree to watch the lavender sea. Inevitably, the dragon would fly wild again. She crushed a plump leaf between her fingers and anointed herself with the juice.

Forehead, throat, wrists. The repetition was soothing, cooling. She could be calmer. She could be better the next time.

Ruby Throated

CALLA RETURNED FROM WORK at the hospital feeling odd, craving release. The neo-natal incubator lamps relentlessly toasted the peaked babies in her care with the unfair truth of life. *You're here now, but this isn't easy.*

It made Calla want to fight with Antonio. *Tell me you might leave. Disrupt us.* She used a nasty tone to chastise him for irritating slights, like forgetting to lock the front door.

"Do you want us murdered in our sleep?"

Antonio was always sketching designs at his drawing table. The dishcloth was always slouched on the kitchen floor.

"This towel sure is heavy," Calla goaded. "I can see why it was too difficult to put back on the hook."

The words were certainly hers but spewed by some inner demon. As soon as she spoke, she felt like a jerk, which generated guilt and other reflections about her shortcomings. The cycle stoked a pleasant fire inside her.

Effortlessly patient, Antonio had none of it. He never screamed back when she taunted, although his hand might pause in the middle of a sweeping, graceful line on the heavy drawing paper. He focused energy instead into the elaborate, baroque flourishes for the custom *Rest in Peace* artwork he sold on decals—the kind mourning family members and friends carefully stuck onto the back windows of their pick-up trucks and four-door sedans.

The work of sadness soaked Calla and Antonio. Perhaps that was what drew them together in the first place.

"How many do you have to finish tonight?" Calla demanded as she came up behind him.

Antonio inked the silhouettes of small black birds in a spiky pattern around lettering.

I am the birds in circled flight. RIP Maria Jones, Mother to all she knew. 1962-2015.

"Just this one."

She felt invisible when he worked.

Antonio found quotes for the decals from Native American prayers for the dead—*one with the universe* type of sentiments. People liked them. Calla glanced at a completed page at the top of the table:

I am with you, I do not sleep. RIP Tomas Cruise 1983-2015.

"Tomas Cruise? Really?"

"Not the actor. Different guy, obviously."

"Probably for the best he's gone. Now he doesn't have to spend the rest of his life dealing with the confusion."

Antonio didn't seem to find any insult or humor in this and denied Calla the reaction she wanted.

"He was pretty young. Did he kill himself? You know, to end the comparisons?"

"I really don't know. Not the sort of thing I ask."

Was he a little ruffled? Maybe she was getting somewhere. She returned to Maria Jones' birds and picked at him again.

"The beaks look too long."

"They're hummingbirds. Did you know you can tell the age of a hummingbird by the width of its beak?"

Antonio's ornithological knowledge surprised Calla and she genuinely asked, "What age are these birds?"

"Hell, I don't know," he laughed. "I have to draw them so tiny that the beaks are all pretty thin, like needles. I suppose these should be adults, mothers maybe, for Maria?" Antonio grabbed Calla's hand, gave the top of it a little peck. She felt a small release.

Calla flopped onto the couch and stared at the beige popcorn ceiling. She thought of painting it sky blue. She remembered something.

"When I was little I saw one in the yard once, hovering over my mother's azalea bush. I thought he might belong to Rumpelstiltskin—that this little bird was his secret and had spun all of the magical golden straw."

"I love your imagination."

Antonio didn't say anything about how hummingbird couples don't nest together, how the females are left alone to build a home and tend babies, because he would never leave Calla by herself to do that. Calla knew about the delicacy of life all too well, so he also didn't tell her that if you hold a hummingbird you must not touch the tiny bone that divides its breast in two or it may go into cardiac arrest.

Instead, he wanted to share a fact of their fortitude, because hope is a gift. "When some hummingbirds migrate, they cross the Gulf of Mexico."

Antonio began to draw more quickly, less carefully, and the hummingbirds grew larger and populated the paper until they covered over Maria Jones' epitaph and flew into one another, crashing at the edges of the pad.

"For two weeks, their wings thrum at near-invisible speeds, over the white caps, while the moon rises and until the sun tugs it down, over and over again."

The figures on the paper furiously rattled the desk and as Antonio finished filling in their growing bodies, they burst forth and darted through the apartment, surrounding him and Calla together in a fabulous, flapping disruption.

Things to Do While Listening to Your Brother on the Phone

USE ACETONE-SOAKED COTTON BALLS to remove chipped nail polish. Mollify him with mirroring-language: Yes. He is afraid to go outdoors. His panic erases him for days. Marvel at the proud little birds outside your window; How do any of us survive the month of February? Press your cheek against the cool glass.

Crouch on the bristling carpet to find grandmother's pearl earrings. Perhaps your memories of a bad childhood are wound into the nests of hair and dust beneath the dresser.

But you are not looking for those.

Tell him you spend a lot of energy not living the past. Tell him it was different for you. Use navy thread and a gleaming needle to mend a ruffled sweater.

He says he thinks he could flee to Bolivia, away from your poisonous family and all of American culture.

Ask him if he has a passport.

Disconnect the edge of thread from its spool with your teeth. You know he will not leave.

In the bathroom, examine the lines around your eyes. You cannot compose your features into a face that looks twenty-five again, when these phone calls began. You share similarities: sadness on cloudy days, guilt for nothing in particular, uneasiness with people. When you listen next Wednesday, walk outside—no matter the cold—and imagine a sun strong enough to sear away his past.

Maps

NO ONE EXPECTED A MAP THIEF to be a girl. No one expected the person extracting antique maps of the ancient worlds from libraries across the northeastern seaboard to be an amateur.

"Have you seen the classic cat burglar movie?" she asked her fiancé, as way of explanation. "The one with Princess Grace and Cary Grant, who wore the hell out of a suit?"

"Weren't they jewel thieves? What about *The Thomas Crowne Affair*? That one seems more like what you do."

She agreed the art heist film was a more logical inspiration. However, when she was ten years old, she had found *To Catch a Thief*'s nighttime scampering across the slated roofs of the Mediterranean irresistible. She dyed her hair platinum to match the princess' blond halo and bought black peg-leg pants. She pretended she had a partner in crime as she snuck through dark stacks of university libraries with an Exact-O blade in her purse.

"Your new look is super hot," her fiancé said, although he remained wary, and refused to join her capers.

He wanted to set a wedding date, but she was too busy to think about floral arrangements and canapés.

Her brother Harry had been on one of those planes that go missing. Not officially down— just missing. Any year now, the authorities expected wreckage to wash up on an Asian shoreline. For two years, Harry had lived somewhere uncharted, between thick cloud cover and physical evidence, and she had been searching for him.

First, the headlines were splashed on red banners across her screens, above images of watery search parties, and she scanned and squinted for Harry's eyeglasses or some other representative object of his person. Then, the story moved to the newspapers where older news goes to fester, and she searched for him eight pages deep within section B, the rattle of paper so satisfying, so physical and tactile in contrast to the lack of fuselage or corpses.

Her boyfriend proposed, hoping the joy of their union might distract her from her grief. Instead of wearing his ring, she had an artist tattoo a compass on the palm of her hand so her body could become a conduit of navigation. She began to look for Harry in maps—nautical, aerial, topographical—she sought them all, initially focusing on modern representations of the assumed crash area. Eventually she became enamored with the historical and beautiful, the gilded, encrusted with age, etched drawings made by cartographers gone for centuries.

It was in the oldest maps where she sometimes caught sight of Harry. He popped up to the surface for a moment with Poseidon, surveyed a whale in the distance, aligned himself with the North Star, and dove back down into the Black Sea. Once she saw him up in the crow's nest of a vast sailboat crossing the Strait of Gibraltar. He waved.

Anytime Harry appeared, she collected him and took him with her. No one misses a folio page from a book of 18th century maps. It was easy in large research libraries where student commotion and space allowed her to sneak a book to a quiet corner and cut. She was clever, kept to the giant atlases, and ignored the pieces hung behind glass on museum walls.

Alone in her apartment on the third anniversary of the plane's disappearance, she watched a special televised documentary about the flight. She lay out all twenty-three maps she'd stolen from four states and poked at circling sharks, hoping for a glimpse of Harry in any condition at all, even half-eaten. She studied the mountains for a tiny hiking Harry, the country borders for signs of his crossing, in the hopes that he had left the seas entirely. Nothing. Not a shred of the 747, not a sign of human movement. A call from her fiancé interrupted her despair.

"I watched your Hitchcock movie. Still looking for a partner in crime?"

With her finger, she traced the O of the Oceannus Indicus on Johannes Honter's 1542 map of Asia, where a few months earlier Harry had done a pull-up on the upper curve of the letter and then slipped back into the blue lines of water.

"Yes," she told him, her spirits afloat.

If she married her fiancé, they could sail the Pacific on their honeymoon. Doubling the size of her private search party might be just the thing.

On the documentary, she half-heard tearful family members of the missing aircraft passengers interviewed as she began plotting visits to new rare map collections. Perhaps they would have luck in the south.

Radioactive

IF YOUR SISTER IS A DRUNK, set the neighborhood Chinese restaurant's ring tone to something cheery, Stevie's "You Are the Sunshine of My Life" maybe, so when the perpetually accommodating owner calls you're in a decent mood for the communique.

"Your sister is here again, telling us about Su Lin. Please come get her?"

Goddamn Su Lin. After one too many Rose often walks to the restaurant to apologize for the 1937 kidnapping of the giant panda cub.

Don't hang with drinkers if you feel invisible when they recite the same story more than once, if it infuriates you that all previous conversations leak through the poorly sealed doors of their minds, if it depresses you that their memories drip out, pool on the floor and spoil.

Ruth Harkness, 1920s self-styled New York socialite, snatched baby panda Su Lin from Sichuan, China, fed him from a baby bottle, and brought him via steam ship across the Pacific to California until he wound up in Chicago at the Brookfield Zoo. He was a bit of an American celebrity.

"Su Lin took photos with Shirley Temple!" Rose will tell you for the thirty-fourth time, as she opens the freezer at my place to chop-chop with a knife at the ice, to drop it plink-plink into a scotch glass. If repetitive sounds churn inside you until they become a mini-tornado slashing and sucking at your heart, don't have a drunk for a sister.

Rose had a baby once she hoped to name Violet. It's hard for me to say if the drinking started before or after she lost her.

Don't have a drunk for a sister if you want to keep your dream job as a zookeeper.

Uninvited, she'll come to see you on Monkey Island at the Brookfield Zoo. If you don't want to spend your days shampooing Labradoodles in a mobile *Pups 'n' Suds* truck parked outside McMansions, keep bottle-rockets and lighters away from your drunk sister. She might give Mrs. Marshall's first grade class an unauthorized education about the monkeys NASA shot into outer space.

When Rose and I emerge from the dark foyer of Mrs. Ma's restaurant, a bag of fortune cookies in hand, Rose tells me a story I haven't heard before. A bunch of French ladies rubbed *Tho-Radia* lotions onto their faces for thirty years in the mid-twentieth century.

"They hoped for a healthy glow when in fact it was radioactive," Rose confides, like it's a government secret.

Rose falls asleep on my couch for the third time this week. The next morning, I feed her coffee and eggs, and she lights a cigarette with her Zippo, examining her face in its chrome mirror.

"Violet was radiant inside me. What good it is to try and glow without her?" If your sister is a drunk, make sure she knows she'll never be alone.

It Grew to a Certain Size

SHE LOVED HOW THE PIG ROCKETED across the living room to her like a firecracker, like a toy car with a haywire remote. It collapsed its legs out to the side, flipped to its back and exposed its vulnerable belly expectantly. When she petted it, the pig grunted in approval and emitted a vibration to make her temporarily at ease with the world.

"You're just a pet," she said.

"Or maybe I'm a trauma pig," it replied.

She handled its floppy ears and wondered if it would hurt the pig to pierce them. It could wear the gaudy rhinestone earrings in the shape of the letter G she'd found while vacuuming her daughter's room.

"Give me a name," the pig said.

She had bought the animal as a piglet from a farm down the road one month after her daughter and the neighbor boy fell through the ice and drowned in the neighborhood retention pond. Surely the pig broke some HOA rule, but no one dared to challenge her. The development was new and, for now, surrounded by cornfields. Drainage was a challenge on the plains and the pond was meant to prevent basements from flooding. Several houses, including her own, encircled the open space into which the pond impressed itself. It had taken only ten unsupervised minutes outside before the children were submerged. When she walked the pig on its leash, she considered how, with so many back windows bearing witness, no one had seen the children venture out onto the frozen surface. No one rushed through their back-patio door to interrupt the terrible idea.

Early on, the pig began dragging its tusks along the walls of the house, marking territory. She didn't mind. As a toddler, her daughter had also left a perimeter of marks three feet off the ground throughout the house as she grasped for balance with hands filthy from exploring—hands soft and hot like sweet rolls. She missed the hair tugging game the two of them had played, where her daughter pulled at her mother's ponytail until she yelled ouch! and the little girl ran away giggling. The chase was the fun. Over time, the anticipation of the yank and the dance of neurons down her spine became pleasurable. *Tug at me again.*

It was when the pig grew to a certain size and ran past her too quickly in the kitchen one day that its tusk made a gash in her leg.

"I still can't believe you didn't get a pygmy," her husband yelled as he threw her a dishtowel.

He insisted at the very least she take the pig back to the farmer to have the tusks cut down.

She wrapped the towel around her calf and realized she needed stitches. The pig smelled the blood and pushed its snout against her.

"I'm a little wild," it said. "But you like it."

The pain was molten and that was a nice contrast to the chilled tendrils grown through her chest.

"I'm sorry," she told the pig. She was being a bad mother again, selfish, shrugging off responsibility.

"I've let things get out of control," she said. Even before the accident she had known she was a worthless type. She never had tissues in her purse or a comb to smooth the flyaways. No emergency mints or god forbid a safety pin to fix a lost coat button. The second her girl was old enough to not require snacks and spare clothing, she stopped carrying a purse at all. Her whole life she had leaned toward the rush of spontaneous problem solving—in a pinch she tore pages out of a nearby magazine to use as a maxi pad. What support would she have been when her daughter reached adolescence anyway?

At the emergency room, fixing the cut on her leg was such a delicate process, the tiny black thread passing back and forth to rejoin the flesh, so unlike all the chaotic pounding and pushing on her daughter. So unlike the forceful intubation that tore at the inside of her girl's throat, the paddles that pulled at her body like magnets whose magic had run out.

That winter day she had allowed her daughter to play with the boy outside while she did chores indoors. At first, she watched them through the kitchen window. They made angels in the open space out back where the snow was mean and bright. Then she moved into the windowless laundry room. Later that night at the hospital, after the children were pronounced dead, she opened her arms repeatedly to mimic how she'd struggled to fold fitted sheets while her daughter and her friend had drowned. With each robotic demonstration, her hand smoothed a sheet that was not there. The boy had been found in the middle of the pond, beneath her daughter. Based on the footprints and the amount of time each child had spent in the water, the police told the families that her daughter had most likely fallen in crossing the ice trying to save the boy.

Had they called out? No one had heard them calling.

Loading the pig into the car was a twenty-minute exercise, which required setting up a small ramp with two-by-fours and some awkward shoving and coaxing of the beast into the backseat. When they arrived, the farmer scolded her as he sedated the pig.

"Trimming is necessary about once a year," he said, as he began sawing at one of the tusks with a special wire.

She named the pig Gabriella.

She placed her hands on Gabriella's belly to feel it slowly rise and fall, and gritted her teeth against the awful sound of the metal through bone while she made circles with her palms, smoothing the white hair.

National Treasure

WHEN ROSE DRANK WHISKEY and the ice tenderly clink-clinked against the glass, the stone inside her dissolved for a while. She felt respectable.

Ms. Baker, the squirrel monkey, also understood difficult circumstances, but made the best of them. NASA had stuffed Ms. Baker into a leather bomber jacket, tucked her into a tiny capsule and slung-shot her into orbit, where she floated above Earth for nine minutes. Rose imagined she looked down at the globe and traced a line showing all she had lost between the Peruvian jungles and Cape Canaveral.

Rose sent a letter to the monkey upon Ms. Baker's return to Earth and subsequent appearance on the cover of *Life*.

"You are a national treasure and you deserve a ticker-tape parade down Fifth Avenue!"

Rose forgave Ms. Baker's lack of reply because of the monkey's many social engagements.

Rose never married, but she had a baby in her for a few weeks, and that was the stone rolling around inside her no one could see. She'd hoped the baby would be a girl but would never know if it was.

Rose's daddy got thrown out of the house more than once for being a sour, jagged drunk.

He nearly killed a man named Norman who flirted with Rose's mother at the grocery store. "You can't blame everything on the war!" her mother had shrieked. Next to the peas in the frozen food aisle, she advised Rose men were nothing but disappointments.

The father of Rose's baby backed away from her at the news of their loss, his arms spread wide in confusion, as if he'd lost any grasp of what he might have possessed. Rose wanted him to step back towards her, prove his love with an embrace and offer her a grand wedding or even just a date at the county clerk's office. She could wear a simple lacey veil. Instead, he turned away, left her pale and shaking, and broke it completely off a few weeks later. Alone in their empty railroad apartment, Rose thought of Ms. Baker's fellow monkey astronaut, Able. She too journeyed to the stars, but died upon re-entry.

Rose's brother worked with the primates at the zoo in Chicago and sometimes when Rose visited, he let her hold one. She almost never drank on zoo days and felt proud about how gentle she could be. Their soft fur in her hands calmed her. She sang to them about Ms. Baker.

Rose's brother shushed her when school trips came through, but Rose refused to be quiet; schoolchildren needed to hear astronaut adventures. She wanted the little monkeys to understand all that was possible, all they could one day become.

Flight Helmet

SHE THINKS ABOUT IT mostly on airplanes, when the pilot deploys the landing gear and the whirring machinery vibrates her seat. Her final wishes stipulate cremation and one day her charred hip replacement socket and ball will be recycled into rivets or significant metal, wings, a rudder. She could affect directional flow. Through scratched plexiglass and misty cirrus, the cars below are toys. She traces where the highways intertwine and kiss. Her metal fillings could become road signs and announce 106 miles to Topeka, or Children Playing.

The six-year old's bicycle had hooked the undercarriage of her car and threw off steering.

All she heard was the scream of another pop song chorus, *baby baby baby*, cheery as the last. She had looked at the radio knobs so briefly. Six was too young for cavities, and the boy had been lucky, never broken a leg, no doctor had screwed metal into bone. He left behind no pieces for wing flaps, no parts to help lift her up.

Nightshade

LAURIE PAINTED A POTATO RED and wore it as a hat to church. The gossip was outstanding and obscured her mother's alarm for Laurie's mental health.

To the Francophile organist, the *pomme de terre* symbolized the apple and Eve, and he applauded Laurie's appropriate concern with original sin. The rector disagreed; Laurie's performance piece spoke to the weight of ungodly acts on the mind. Because the Spirit moves through the heart, keeping the tuber close the chest, perhaps with a baby carrier, would be an improvement. The eleven-year old acolyte prayed the potato would roll off when Laurie bowed for the Gospel reading. Imagine the thump! The red slime on the carpet! But Laurie had carefully threaded a ribbon through the hat and well-secured it to her head.

Laurie's color choice disgusted the coffee hour hostess. The scalloped potatoes waiting for the congregation in the kitchen hall were now wholly unsavory. The woman who brought up the offering worried about paint fumes and the danger to Laurie and those sitting in the pews around her. Had she used a nontoxic paint? Nail polish? The sheen was arresting.

During the Prayers of the People Laurie's boyfriend guiltlessly wondered if she would continue to have sex with him after what they had done with the baby.

At the communion rail, Laurie untied the bow at her chin, and the potato slid over her bangs and into her cupped palms with the satisfying weight of a bunny rabbit or a snow globe.

The rector approached with the sacrament, and Laurie whispered, "This is my love, which I give unto you for safekeeping. It is too soft for the fierce world and I cannot be trusted."

Baby Dreams

AS HER BODY SWELLS with the baby, her dreams become strange and of dysmorphia.

Grotesque bat wings hang from the underside of her arms and her thighs are too wide for chairs. In the mornings she checks the mirror, certain it will reflect a leathery creature too enormous for flight.

Other dreams are somewhat less alarming. She enjoys normal moments with her husband, like folding laundry, petting flat the pockets on his shirt before hanging it on his side of the closet. He laughs at something the NPR program host says but her thoughts are muddy and she does not understand the joke. Dreams shift to lust, honey-warm and delightful. Her husband plays with her hair but the baby pounds his fists, a rhythmic code of high alert. The man is no longer her husband. The transgression confuses her but they kiss and she does not want to stop and feels no guilt. Is it cheating if she's been tricked, if it feels so good?

She takes long walks in the hope exercise will ensure dreamless sleep. Stretching her legs relieves the increasing weight on her pelvis. To the west, the front range of the Rocky Mountains lift their flat slabs of rock from singed grass. Sunlight hits her shoulders like beams from a child's invisible stingray gun and she longs for the night. All summer she forgets sunscreen and a water bottle. She huffs around the neighborhood in flip-flops and wipes a sweaty hand on the dress she has repurposed and knotted beneath her stomach. The hypnotizing swirls of purples and yellows on the fabric are not her style, but pregnancy allows her to play dress-up—everything is masquerade now.

The water meter man catches her attention with his neon orange vest and portable radio, its blare scattering small animals. A squirrel perched in a nearby fir flicks its tail angrily and in a litany of clicks, lectures on the terror of high frequencies to those with excellent hearing. The man stalks through lawns, disappears behind houses, and emerges to enter data in a hand-held device. She wonders to whom he returns at night and if that person minds his intimacy with so many homes. She wraps her forearms around the bottom of her belly as if she could elevate it, imagines hoisting it with helium balloons like the house in a kid's movie.

Her thirst is like the recurring dream she had as a virginal girl, where she met a man walking along a beach. When their bodies joined, she was convinced the sensation of their union was accurate and it would feel the same when it happened in waking life. Later she discovered, if anything, the dream sex amplified reality.

"Hey there mamma. Watch your step."

A young workman kneels in the grass. He smooths a section of freshly poured sidewalk with a metal dowel. When she tries to pull her left foot from the concrete, the flip-flop makes a sucking sound.

She raises her foot to inspect the clinging gray sludge. "Yes, well," he smiles. "Too late."

She loses balance and the man catches her elbow. The skin on his palm is rough. "Do you want to sit?"

"I'm fine." She taps at her belly, forces a laugh.

He rises to stand, still cupping her elbow. She leans forward and kisses him, but only briefly, because the baby kicks her bladder, signaling she is awake.

"Stay," the man says, and he quickly draws a heart into the wet cement.

She cannot. Her skirt becomes a sail and she uses her wings to lift into the air, her concrete-covered foot an awkward difficulty, but she rises.

Yes vs. No

SHE WAS FLIRTATIOUS IN JULY, wearing yes like a feverish new skin, leading with her hips, wearing her hair high off her neck. Because of the way her curls framed her aquiline nose, men told her she looked like a painting from long ago, but they never understood her. A beefy Australian with barbed wire tattoos invited her to sit on his lap and asked, "Are you a mother?" As if she were old enough for that.

Boredom felt criminal so she went dancing alone when necessary. She wore a long silky skirt and an indecent top that revealed her bra straps the night a Russian architecture student picked her up.

"You don't look like you belong here. You are too classy for this place." His accent had complex structure. He was wrong and right. She was playing dress-up.

"I'll take you somewhere better."

They met the next Friday at a French bistro with white tablecloths, classy enough to include the actress Isabella Rossellini, who sat nearby. Later that weekend she would pick up extra waitressing shifts to cover her half of the bill, images from the weird sex scenes in David Lynch films haunting her while she served lobster fra diavolo to an elderly man on supplemental oxygen. A jazz trio played while she and the Russian dined. His bright eyes and dark hair almost made up for the crooked teeth and dull conversation. With his fingertips, he lightly brushed her knuckles and she liked how he played with the gold bangles on her arm. But it all seemed like some kind of business transaction. When they left the restaurant, she pulled away when he leaned in for a kiss.

"Would you like to see my apartment?" He asked gravely, as if offering entrance to his soul. Embarrassed for him, she agreed.

He shared a loft with two other students and was proud of the bunk bed he had constructed to fit over his drafting desk. Among the linear drawings of building exteriors, she noticed a sketch of a naked woman with dimensions like hers. It was quite good. He touched her shoulder, but the awkwardness was palpable, the arrangement unnatural. After driving her home, he again moved to kiss her. This time she let him. Maybe she could overlook the poor dentistry, force her way through the uncertainty.

Over the weeks, he called and called, and with each message he left, she became more convinced of her disinterest. It shouldn't be so hard to like a person.

"No," she told him. She was not custodian of her heart.

He pinned a terrible letter to her door calling her a whore. The vengeful threats in all capital letters included a story of another woman he had beaten up.

SHE DID NOT TREAT ME AS POORLY.

No. She rejected his false passion.

He woke her up late one night, banging. "Are you home? Open!"

Hiding beneath the down comforter she had saved to buy when she was eleven, she wished for physical transparency, to become a ghost. She would have to shed her summer skin.

Fat Girl Lament

THE CEILING OF THE JAZZ BAR in Vienna is painted with stars like the domes of the gothic churches Janie visits to pray for a night like this. At a trumpet bleat he presses his leg against her. The universe above them peels in gold and blue flakes and he is a jackal but any animal will do. Janie's had a few drinks and finds it all vaguely romantic, this cathedral to inevitability and imperfection. She closes her eyes to the constellations and decides to sleep with him.

On the bed with her skirt pulled to her waist, she imagines herself a disjointed, angular subject of an Egon Schiele sketch hung on a museum wall. He kisses her fleshy back and she remains a Botticelli, but it is as good a time as any to feel beautiful. His desire makes her beautiful. All her life she has prayed for desire as deliberate as this.

When she awakens, it's not much past dawn, and he's already up, scooping instant coffee into a mug. She smiles at him, and he looks her over, then breaks the silence with an offering of thanks for her lustiness, a good time when feeling low. He goes back to making coffee for himself without asking if she wants any. He pulls on his jeans.

Janie feels the night receding, a familiar tug downward. He takes milk from the refrigerator, and she notices the pop art postcard she taped to the door weeks ago. Sigmar Polke's topless *3 Girls* pose, hands on hips, pushing their boot heels into a man's back. The man's mouth is open, he's saying something, but the girls aren't looking down or listening. They grin and hold their chins high.

When she is alone again, Janie will watch snow collect in puddles illuminated by elegant streetlamps. She will write a sappy poem about the night and then crush it underfoot.

The Girl and the Fox Pirate

AFTER HOURS AT THE MUSEUM, the Fox and I lean back on the spinning-bench beneath the famous artist's blown glass installation. All the cranky mothers and their children are gone and the lights are low. The seat glides on its circular track and the sculpted world suspended above hypnotizes. Babies and tiny shells, snakes and cerulean orbs, all lit from the atrium above. The colors smear across our bodies and paint us beautiful.

"Lean here," the Fox says, hooking me close. He guides my head to the steady rhythm in his chest.

In the children's theater, he plays a pirate. Last year he was a fox who advised the turtle on racing the hare. Negative splits, track suits, go baby, go. He auditioned for the hare but couldn't escape his sexiness. I have loved him from the beginning. Between acting jobs, he paints houses and landscapes, and dreams of making it to Broadway.

"Let's never stop." I hum to accompany a far-away song.

"You spin me right round baby." The Fox laughs into my hair and pulls me onto his lap, puts his hands around my waist. He says he wants to ride the carousel on the top floor.

I am a jack-of-all-trades at the museum. When I usher theater shows, taking tickets and pointing out the stroller parking area, I watch my Fox strut. Other days I prowl the preschool wing and repair the waterscapes the babies clog with pacifiers. I don't mind sweeping micro-fine grains from the floor at the sand table, because of the way the children giggle when they throw the glittery stuff into the air again.

Under the rainbow light, I lean down and kiss his nose and mouth, before I hop off for a fox chase up the ramp and out of the basement. We run ourselves dizzy along the winding trail ascending the atrium, marveling at the sculpture's inferno of reds and oranges at the very top. On the near-ancient carousel, lions and tigers lurk in the darkness. I recite the scripted safety speech the carousel chaperone typically makes through the loudspeaker. You must be at least three years old to ride an animal alone, etc. I refuse to blare the carnival music, which tests the sanity of every parent and employee. The volume is fixed. My favorite part of carousel duty is when I insert my hand into the monkey puppet to dazzle the children. Strapped to their rams and zebras they watch, mouths agape, while the monkey claps his cymbals to the drum's beat.

The Fox and I push the power button and the machinery creaks as the carousel gets to cruising speed.

"I want to defile you on this beast." He points to the tiger's shellacked stripes. I am unconvinced. "Maybe instead on one of the little benches?"

But I think better of it. While checking the belt on a hyperactive child, I once overheard a mother, nursing her infant on a bench, confess to another woman her husband's interest in drinking her milk. "Directly from my breast!"

The carousel is the least sexy of all places.

The Fox winks at me. "Come on. This thing makes me hot," he says in a pirate accent. "This is sacred space," I tease.

Could he really make it in New York? He is young and living in his hometown to be near his sister, who is continuously sick with a childhood cancer she can't shake even though she is no longer a child. He is a good person and if she dies, he will not stay for me. It's okay. He might be talented enough.

He sighs, his smile a charm. He will get what he wants, eventually. We've made out in the family bathroom near the dinosaur exhibit, where the framed vintage posters on the walls above the toilets are of ominous monster movies like *The Land That Time Forgot* and *Behemoth the Sea Monster*. "Monsters launch attack against earth," he whispers, his arms welcome tentacles moving across me.

I wave him over to a pair of extravagantly painted horses performing their chaste pole dance. The Fox climbs onto the white one next to mine, and we hold hands across the space between them.

One day I will leave this place and become a teacher or go to veterinary school, or maybe I will stay here forever and become Director of New Programs. For now, we pretend the tiny electric lights puncturing the ceiling really are stars. The horses gallop in ever-widening circles until we are absorbed by the night itself and become our own galaxy of twitching desire.

Sexpot Mermaid

"HEAR FROM YOUR MOM?" I squeezed the steering wheel to flex, hoping Meg would notice.

"Nothing."

She focused on the edge of an ice cream sandwich and violently flipped through a *Rolling Stone*. I keep a few magazines tucked under the seat—selling ice cream makes for long days. I didn't ask why she was dipping into the wares at ten am after she'd complained the day before about getting fat; the wisest thing my brother Tony ever told me is sometimes you've got to *keep your trap shut*.

"She'll come around," I assured Meg. Her mom would get over the fact Meg had moved in with me.

Sometimes moms just need time. Mine was already improving. After Tony was killed in Iraq she didn't get out of bed for months, but when Meg and I left the house that morning to play handball, my mom was sitting up on the couch, watching television.

Meg licked her fingers, threw the magazine to the floor of the truck. "It's not about patience with her. You know she wants me to commit to being a musician and to avoid the mistakes she made with men. She thinks I'm failing at both."

My mom only ever cared if we finished school and were good guys. Tony did both and he's dead. I'm selling weed out of the truck on the side. I still think I'm still a pretty good guy though.

I parked along the chain-link fence at my old junior high school and scanned for the kid who sometimes met me there to buy a joint. Thankfully it was too early for him to be out of bed. Meg did not approve of my side business.

I kissed her on the neck, gave her a squeeze as we walked across the yard to the handball court. Pieces of hair from her ponytail caught in my mouth.

"My mom's compulsive about her music. I'm not like that."

Meg's better than she thinks, maybe better than her mom, and actually is obsessed with the cello. When she goes on about her vibrato not being steady enough and her sloppy plucking I don't really follow so I stay quiet and nod. Her sexy, messy eyeliner easily distracts me.

Just shut up and listen, Tony always said.

It's what I do with mom when she misses him. Sometimes we sit on the couch at night, watch an old movie, and she tells stories back when she thought life would keep going in a certain direction. She reminds me of things Tony did when he was little, even before Dad died. I stay quiet.

"There she is, our favorite girl," Meg pointed to the concrete wall wrecked with graffiti.

She knew my fondness for a particularly well drawn, double-life-size mermaid in the right-hand corner. My sexpot mermaid wore a lippy smile and her red hair flowed down to shimmery green hips. Meg and I sometimes played for extra points if we managed to hit one of her hot pink nipples. Meg's cool that way.

I pulled a ball out of my pocket and aimed for the mermaid's face, trying to navigate the cracks in the asphalt underfoot.

Meg sat on a crumbling bench. "I want to know how it works." She meant selling weed, a secret I had admitted after a recent close call with the police.

I ran the business out of the ice cream truck after a few months of smoking a little every now and then to help me sleep. I could have told Meg it kept the nightmares about Tony away. She knew about the bad dreams but she didn't understand, not really.

"The less you know, the better."

She had listened to me explain why I rode the ferry alone late at night. She'd heard my descriptions of the peace I feel when I lean over the side, stare at the black water, and wait for the harbor to reflect lights when the boat pulls in to dock. Back in high school Tony and I used to ride together every weekend, head out to clubs or ball games in the Bronx or just wander, endlessly walking the city. Meg didn't have any siblings, hadn't lost anyone.

I knocked the ball against the wall a few more times until I realized someone had messed with my mermaid. Closer up I could see the side of her lip curled with new ink. Filthy words marched out of her mouth, spiky, impure insects. She wasn't mine any more. I snatched the ball and stormed away, back toward the truck.

"We'll fix it!" Meg called after me. "We can paint over it, make repairs!"

I kept walking. It had been stupid to think she could keep me afloat. So much was beyond repair.

Young Blood

IN THE SEVENTH GRADE Carina wears a turquoise tank top to her first girl-boy party, and her hair is long and shiny and she'll never feel so pretty again. When two boys from another school serenade her—*My Girl*—Carina hands over her tangy little heart. They split it between them, tear it right down the middle seam and then roll the pieces up to tuck into the back pockets of their blue jeans, where they hold them hostage for a year or two. Sometimes they all meet up after school on Fridays and wander the East Village for hours, woozy from hormones surging through their vessels. When the boys direct their scattershot attention at Carina, she is lush with sensations prickly and foreign.

Carina's mother draws blood at the hospital and runs her fingers over Carina's arm.

Oooh, her mother teases, *what a nice, plump vein, a gorgeous vein,* and she empties the paraphernalia from her lab coat pockets onto her dresser. When Carina is alone sneaks into her mother's bedroom and ties the thick rubber band around her arm until she quivers, disgusted. The empty vials are so light in her hand, the stoppers that plug the ends red and spongey.

One of the beautiful, genius boys who sang to Carina grows up and develops a degenerative disease that kills him by forty. There is no reason to believe he ever thought about Carina as his life became a complicated mission, filled with wheelchairs and activism. But he hadn't returned his half of her heart in the same condition she gave it to him, so his spirit pulls at her dreams for a while. She mourns.

In her own middle age Carina is a sedated wild thing, a trained falcon usually wearing her hood. When she is free, it is a caffeine-fueled affair, a dance party in the kitchenette of a suburban box squatting among hundreds, her body pumping with a secret confidence. She indulges in these occasional love affairs with herself, hopping and writhing, joyful with her ample thighs, soft breasts. She speaks her desires aloud.

Carina volunteers to assist in shark dissection for her son's fifth grade class because in adulthood one must find ways to be brave. With a pictorial she and the children identify the gill slits and fins on the exterior of the rubbery, gray body. The caudal fin is the one that propelled the shark through the water, where it was able to detect a drop of blood from a football field away. Carina pries open the mouth with a pencil to inspect the teeth and she hums a tune from a movie her son and classmates have never seen.

The children are unwilling to use the scalpel to cut into the shark, which is a female and has been drained of blood. Who can blame them when they are so young and not yet ready? She looks at their perfectly smooth faces and wishes there were a way to bathe her bursting, aged heart in their young blood to shrink it to a more effective size. Lately its swollen beat and habit of seizing at every stupid-sad television commercial feels like new evidence of a known design flaw. If the shark is pregnant with pups, its vascular system will be robust to support new life.

Before making the first incision, Carina whispers to it, *We will dissect your liver and brain, but I will protect your tiny heart, and put it my pocket to remember you.*

Our Grief is a Receipt
of Our Love

ALICE'S MOTHER IS TERMINALLY ILL and as is the custom, the whole family will be lethally injected and buried together in a cemetery by the sea. On her last day, Alice takes her final shower and grieves all the books she will never read, paintings she will never see, music she will never hear. Rushing to the beach, her billowy dress catches at her legs and she worries her wet hair will mold in her grave. An administrator tells the family once they are poisoned, long metal rods will force their spines straight. Alice's mother does not cry.

Alice's foot hits the brake pedal like a bass drum, but she cannot stop the Pontiac and she will kill them all. Her mother remains calm in the passenger seat, even while children squeal in the back. As the station wagon tips over the cliff, the waterfall claims all sound.

At an inspirational talk, Alice asks the best-selling author how to believe in a God who allows the kind of pain she feels in the loss of her mother. The speaker says our grief is a receipt of our love. Everywhere we go we must wave the fluttering papers above our heads as evidence of our wondrous lives.

In the bruised night, the four posters of Alice's bed transform into erect, red-eyed demons. Her baby screeches next to her, a creature growing fangs sharp enough for this world. Alice falls back asleep with arms outstretched, fingertips drumming the headboard. In the morning, the tingle from her pinched nerves promise she will never escape fear.

Cheerleader

ALL SUMMER PAUL LEFT ME IN BED to take his brother Tony's combat helmet for late night drives in the ice cream truck. He woke me at three am to report he'd parked on the hill, hypnotized by the city's glitter, after riding the ferry through the blackness.

"I'm awake now. I'm revved up," he'd say, wanting sex.

Some mornings I woke up alone and I climbed up from the room we shared in his mom's basement to find her in her usual spot on the couch, watching cable, wearing her purple robe. Her coarse mess of reddish-toned hair sprouted from two inches of graying roots. I vowed I'd never let myself go.

"Did you hear about the cheerleader in Maui?" she once asked in her slow, medicated voice. She only talked to me to tell a death story.

"I haven't."

I never knew whether to encourage the stories or switch the subject when she talked sad. Tony had died at the start of the year and Gina rarely left the house or did much at home. I had peeked into Tony's bedroom and it was obvious she no longer cleaned it—the spider webs between the weight set on the floor and the little league trophies on the dresser were all part of the shrine. A poster of Derek Jeter curled at the edges, his face half sun-bleached.

"Hawaii this time. Bad things happen *everywhere*, Megan," Gina warned, slurring the last words together.

"I suppose so."

My desire for Paul to materialize during these conversations burned down to my toes. I hated comforting Gina alone, because when Gina cried, she made sounds like she was strangling.

She turned back to the television, her fingers finessing Tony's cross around her neck. "The cheerleader fell from a ninth-floor hotel balcony."

Gina began trolling the news for stories about kids dying when Tony left for war and it only worsened when he died.

She tucked her legs underneath her robe. "They found the girl naked! Absolutely nothing on. Fell into a bush."

"Wow."

I wondered how much longer Paul would be away.

Gina waved her fingers. "Two boys in the room but the cops questioned them and let them go. I bet they pushed her."

"Do you really think so? Maybe she was just drunk and fell."

"Maybe."

Gina turned back to the TV and started to cry. "Her poor mother."

Would my mother care if I fell off a balcony in Maui? If I didn't begin school at the conservatory in a few weeks as planned, I'm not sure she'd care about me ever again. Since I'd moved in with Paul, I'd stopped answering her frantic calls. Now they had stopped all together.

I thought I loved Paul but he only wanted to have sex after the city had beckoned him away from me. More and more when

I shut my eyes as Paul moved on top of me I saw Tony's face, even though I'd never met him. I was becoming as fixated on his absence as Paul and Gina. It felt spiritual but also wrong.

After sex, we usually had trouble falling asleep. Paul probably thought about the hidden places where fallen buildings and brothers go and I listened to his fast breathing and the ice cream truck humming outside the basement window, trying to make some kind of pattern or a song out of it. Was I any help at all, to anyone? My left hand wandered along the phantom bridge of my cello as I willed away images of Tony torn apart by the roadside bomb. I missed wrapping my arms around the wood of my instrument and coaxing out its deepest notes, the dark ones, to warm me.

Give Me Your Hand
and I Will Pull You Up

GIRLS IN TROUBLE throw the best parties. For her thirtieth birthday Tori flounced about her crowded apartment in a white silk dress with enormous dots, her breasts marked by the black circles like askew targets. For amusement, Martin imagined surreptitiously throwing cashews at them later in the night— once Tori was too drunk to discern their origin. Martin hadn't been invited to the party, but he had information to share: as of last week, three of the four women he'd slept with in his life were now dead. Tori was in danger.

His ex-girlfriend smiled benevolently over her enormous cake ablaze with candles, unaware of Martin's presence. He looked up at the winking string lights above, which he imagined Tori had nailed into the molding earlier in the day. He pictured her tottering on heels on a stepladder, steadied by her new lover Tom, accidentally cracking the plaster with a hammer. She was notorious for stupid shit, for carelessly wreaking destruction. Martin would rather slice his throat with the knife Tori waved over the cake than shake hands with this new person she was associating with.

He had watched Tom all night. Tom was the sort of man who wore tight rust-colored jeans and his blond hair in a bun. Tom was the sort of preening ass who scattered giggling women like sparrows when he moved from one room to the next. Above the din of hip-hop and the racket of dancing and talking, Martin's heart buzzed with hatred. All her life Tori had waded through a rising flood of trouble. Martin was the one walking through it to rescue her, a circus-man on stilts, holding a hand out to pull her up, waiting for her to look up at him with those golden eyes. He had to warn Tori of her precarious position in his list of lovers.

Ah, but here was Tom, appearing behind the birthday girl, pressing himself against her to ease her knife-wielding arm down into the dessert, as if they were now wed. As if this was the jovial cake-throwing photo opportunity at a ballroom reception. Tori and Tom, Tom and Tori!

Martin opened the palm of his hand and began smacking himself in the face. Gently at first, then harder. He had to warn her. He didn't know how it might happen. Maybe this knife portended violence? He feared he had become the devil hiding in the shadows, bringing death to all he loved.

Death 1. Maria, his high school girlfriend, hit by a van while jogging.

Death 2. Jen, his college girlfriend, "fell" off her apartment roof in South Korea.

Death 3: Shania, his main squeeze before Tori, listened too attentively to the voices in her head.

At the news of Shania's death Martin became certain this line of misfortune was a clear pattern. Tori was next.

The lovebirds were laughing, smearing pink frosting and kissing, passing the creamy stuff back and forth on their tongues for everyone to see. Disgusting. Martin's hand moved more violently against his head.

How could he warn her? The people around him had stopped dancing, ignoring the rumbling bass line. They noticed his ineptitude, his inability to keep Tori safe. He was raving, both of his hands now getting in on the action, wildly smacking his forehead, his neck, moving up to pull at his hair. The guests possibly thought he was having a fit or losing his mind. But Martin was simply repressing the urge to push through the hipster crowd of fedoras and flat-sandals, bespectacled-men with beards, girls with hair tied in elaborate braids, and take the knife away.

Wedding Season

AT THE RECEPTION the dance floor divides tables of guests into young and old. For the first time we are assigned to sit with the aged, but it is right and so. We are not the punk couple with sculpted cheekbones wearing suede heels, or the mustached-man in a vest grinding with a wisp in a mini-dress. We replace water-heaters and pay for third-grade textbooks. We are snails, our shells the consequence of time. They are our burden, our strength, our curated selves. We tuck ourselves into them at night.

Ensconced in the shadows, wearing sensible eveningwear, we peer around riotous dahlias blocking our view to everything, to each other. But we cannot escape the lanky bride and her earnest groom. They bewitch us all in the photographer's lights.

"I can't eat this shrimp," says the pregnant woman in red next to me.

"I once ate so much seafood the soles of my feet turned black," her husband says, taking her plate.

"That color certainly announces her condition," twitters the woman to my left, nodding toward the pregnant woman. Some of us are wary of the emboldened.

The disc jockey calls the wedding party to the floor and they rustle across the parquet in sage and cream satins, the camera forcing unnatural pauses in their cavorting, breaking the rhythm. We were like that once, losing step in the lightness of youth. When we are invited to dance it will be in celebration of the span of time we ourselves have been married. The crowd will give a standing ovation to the couple who has survived their vows the longest.

I flirt with the mercury-poisoned husband over dinner and then, later, with his wife, whose violet eyes are as distracting as her swollen belly. When we dance, she touches the small of my back, in the place where my shell is most tender.

"All is not lost," she says into my ear, and I want to believe her. We wave to our spouses on the other side of the floor.

At the end of the night, we each take home a slice of cake in a tiny paper box shaped exactly to fit its content.

I See the Way Your Eyes Follow Me at Target

I WOULD GUESS YOU DID NOT write a poem in your head about us like I did while you made a jump-shot in the middle school gymnasium to impress me. We are too old for this, trading glances at Kids Sports Camp, beneath the singeing light of suburban box stores, at the charming town playground, towing our collections of children along like trophies, like props.

You are dark and lean and I imagine your mother speaks to you in Russian. I could climb you, a chubby squirrel nesting at the first frost.

Underwater

TRISH WOULDN'T CARE if he was late coming home again if he pulled a Cheever and swam. Probably no one had thought of this before in their fly-over suburban town—probably no one had even read *The Swimmer*. He waved the bartender to settle up, said one last thing about the game to the guy on the next stool, and slouched out of the place in somewhere between ten seconds and twenty minutes. The spring evening drizzled but he would be really wet soon enough so it didn't matter. As he scuffled along the sidewalk, his fingers smoothed away droplets from tulip tree flowers. He cupped the petals gently in his palm. Trish having the baby split him open with tenderness.

At the end of Main Street, he found a house with a backyard pool but the cover was fastened tight. It was March and snowed just last week so, of course, no one in town had opened their pools, but the jig was not up! He made breaststroke motions with his arms through heavier rain, and swam for a while, alternating between sidestroke and crawl, a few blocks up and over to the high school.

Inside the Aquatics Center he pushed past the annoying kid who pointed at the wall clock and said the pool wasn't open for community swim past 8pm. Trish would only find his coming home late funny if he Cheever-ed it, so he dove in without paying and warm water filled the pockets of his gray suit. He sunk quickly, pulled down by dress shoes and the new baby's eight pounds—a weight he'd never be able to put down. At the bottom, it was bliss but he didn't stay long before the annoying kid had him under the armpits and they shot up like rockets to the surface.

During the awkward scramble up onto the tiles, he elbowed the boy in the nose to wrestle free and escaped to the locker room. He slammed the door of a pink stall and sat on the toilet to relax and squeeze out his cuffs. This was the women's room and it was graffitied with loopy script in purple and black markers.

Who else thinks the boy who cleans over here is cute?
God, he is so cute!
Girl, yes. I thought I was the only one!
And he has beautiful eyes.
He is even cuter now with green hair. 😊
LOL.

Everything was so pink, and he cried, thankful Trish hadn't done that to the baby's nursery. His mother's pink Mary Kay Cadillac wore aggressively spiky rubber eyelashes, which protruded from the front headlights, announcing her success, humiliating him when he had been in high school. Water dripped from his pant legs in a pattern like his mother's nails tapping on the steering wheel while she made sales calls. His foot shook involuntarily. Right after the baby arrived his mother stopped by unannounced, overly-fragrant and benevolent with twenty shares of company stock for her granddaughter and for Trish, a discount certificate for a local weight loss center.

For a year after he graduated from college, he had lived with his mother before he found an office job. Just to piss her off he worked at the middle school on the janitorial staff and dyed his hair blue.

It was like time had folded in on itself and the girls' bathroom graffiti conversations were all about him.

He dug a pen out from his jacket pocket to respond.

Y'all are cute too.

P.S. Mary Kay kissing lip gloss in Cherry Red is a hot color.

The gin was wearing off and he knew the cops would be coming for him, hopefully to give him a warning and take him home. When he got there, he imagined picking Trish up and swinging her around, but he wasn't as strong as he used to be with all the hours sitting at the office, and she was still plump from the pregnancy. He considered the night a success, however, because for a second when he was under water, he had seen a future of tea parties with his daughter and one day she would be writing about boys on bathroom stalls and marry some guy who hid from her in bars. Or, it would be different for her, and she would be the one hiding.

The Motherhood Gig

MARLEE DESERVED EVERY BAD THING NOW, insomnia included, for abandoning her child. The streetlamp formed a phantom orb behind her eyelids as she thought about her last day with Henry, who she had left crying in his crib, punishment for needing her more than she could stand. She'd fought for air as she tromped through the small house, her son's voice wailing fire engine arpeggios. She blamed Jack for insisting she have the baby she never wanted, for believing they could ever be a sweet family. She had hit her head against the bathroom tiles, wanting the pain to clear the mess she'd made. Oh, what Henry took— her breast, her touch, her voice. In the day, Jack left them to work, and most nights he rehearsed with the band for which Marlee once sang. She suffocated. To survive she had fled across the country a few weeks ago, back to an old boyfriend in Boston. She wanted to sing her life on stage again.

Marlee dragged herself to the T to meet a friend from her days at the college of music. A pregnant woman hauled herself up the steep trolley stairs and a man near the door offered up his seat. The woman placed her hand on her giant belly and Marlee remembered Henry's stillness until the very end of the pregnancy when he flipped around like a fish, fins knocking Marlee's ribs up high on the left.

The train whisked them out of the darkness and up into the green corridor of Fenway where the pregnant woman closed her eyes to the light. As their speed increased, so did Marlee's sense of disconnection. She wanted to take it all back, to be a different person, not stronger, just capable of balance.

Though it was not her stop, Marlee impetuously followed the pregnant woman off the train in Brookline. They walked single file along a field scattered with children playing soccer until the woman disappeared through the glass doors of an aquatics center. Marlee dashed up three flagstone steps behind her. Inside, the lobby window provided a view of a large, old swimming facility. A teenager sat at the desk.

"Adult lap swim goes for another hour. Five dollars."

Marlee checked the large clock on the wall. She was almost late for lunch. She could always say the trains were slow.

"I'm not here to swim. Can I go in and sit on the bleachers?"

"Whatever. Take your shoes off, though."

A wave of chlorine hit Marlee when she opened the door. She made her way across the slippery tiles and waited. She wanted the pregnant woman to give her a sign. She wanted instructions on how to behave.

In the wading pool three ladies tapped their hands on the water's surface to a private rhythm. They waggled their armpits over kickboards and fluttered white feet. The pregnant woman emerged from the locker room, wearing a blue halter-top barely covering her belly. She braced herself on the steel railing to the wading pool.

A lady in a hydrangea-patterned bathing suit peppered her with questions. "Boy or girl? How far along? Is it your first? What hospital?"

The pregnant woman answered rapidly and too softly for Marlee to hear. Marlee thought she didn't want to talk but simply to float and be left alone.

A woman in a nubby white bathing cap said, "I envy the life you have before you," and kicked away.

The pregnant woman smiled politely and closed her eyes to float, her stomach a small island protruding from the chlorine sea. As if it were a contagious action like a yawn, Marlee also closed her eyes and sunk into the thick air until she too was submerged in a refreshing lack of thought and feeling. Each swish and smack of the pool water against the tiles lapped away at her guilt.

Just as the humidity began to make her woozy, Marlee's phone vibrated with a text about an audition that evening. She leaned against the sweating cinderblock wall, her heart banging around. She would go, knock them out, get the gig. The pool's aroma tripped an olfactory memory of Marlee painting. She had stood on a ladder in Henry's room and reached with a brush to dot the blue ceiling with white clouds.

"I can do this," she told Jack, back when she was a force of pretending. "And it doesn't matter if it's a boy or a girl."

"I'm here if you fall," he said. Jack was gooey with love.

Despite everything, he deserved more than the brief, shitty note she left him.

Motherhood was a constant fall, a never-ending tumble. After she'd finished her nursery fresco and looked for surprise shapes in her sky, Marlee couldn't find any meaning in the edges and swirls she created.

Was it even motherhood anymore, once she'd left?

The phone buzzed again with the time and location for the audition. "Yes, I'll go!"

Everyone in the pool turned towards Marlee's shout and she waved vigorously at the pregnant woman, who returned the enthusiasm with weak-wristed confusion. Marlee quickly tiptoed out of the pool. She was half an hour late for lunch. She madly texted her friend about the potential gig. She was unstoppable, powered by the sun, convinced every choice she'd made led to this opportunity.

But at the station, when Marlee climbed into the trolley, she felt a phantom ache flipping around inside of her for Henry, poor unwanted Henry. She missed the warm, sweet smell of his head and the way he clutched at her finger when he nursed at her breast. A snippet of fondness. It was mostly terrible. She wasn't one of those women who could smother her baby with the handmade purple quilt hanging on the wall over the crib, or someone who floors the Volvo so it plunges the whole brood over a highway overpass, but she understood women who do such things. She'd stepped off a cliff, believing Jack when he promised she could be a mother to his baby and continue to sing in their band.

"You nurse and rock him to sleep tonight so I can go sing with the Spurs tonight," she'd cried, but nothing was so easy.

"He won't go down for me, honey," Jack said. "He needs you."

On the rare night Jack agreed to take care of his son, Marlee removed motherhood like a black tank top after a sweaty session under the stage lights, but it wasn't enough. The band replaced her. She sang Jack's alt-country songs to an audience of one and hungered for the weight of the guitar against her hip.

Standing in the first trolley car with a view to the world rushing past, Marlee promised herself she would call Jack soon to better explain. She wouldn't mind if he came to visit her with Henry. She would ask forgiveness and remind him of what she had told him when they first met.

When Marlee was a child herself and ran wild in the tall backyard grasses her mother nagged, "My little butterfly, you need to stop your flitting about and hang the laundry."

Marlee had said, "Mama, I'm a songbird today, and I have too many songs to sing to hang your undies on the line."

The Wolves Within

By 10 P.M. WE'LL BE TUCKED TIGHT in suburbia, thirty miles north of this downtown dive bar, long before Punk Night begins. Our friends and their jam band are the early openers so we'll be well rested for tomorrow's soccer practices or spinning classes, donning rain boots and fleece, or spandex and fitness gadgets that tell us when we've worked off tonight's beers. This is who we are now. I've had a few and I'm investigating the geometric floor tiles. The pattern is the same as the floors of every institutional place I've been—my junior high bathroom, a church kitchen— and those places were primers for being here, where the ceiling is painted black and the bartender is grumpy. A punk kid with a neck tattoo, maybe twenty-five, walks past smelling like strawberries, and he goes outside to smoke, which is not a sweet habit but right then I would follow him anywhere. The way he tilts his head when he talks to the bouncer, the way he flexes his bicep, the way he is young and wired, reminds me of someone I loved long ago. I spin on my stool and watch shadows on the faces of my middle-aged friends under the stage lights, red, yellow, blue. I went to a gallery opening three years ago in New Orleans showing the usual art and wire sculptures, but also custom-made, vaguely S&M leather goods modeled by a lovely woman. $300 for a soft brown breastplate connecting to a suede collar and a harness. $150 for a braided belt attached to a tasseled leash. I nearly gave the leather artist my measurements but what I really wanted was to purchase the last fifteen years. The band plays one of their best tunes and I am still here in my body and can my old lover hear music where he is, does he commune with David Bowie's matter, do they now reverberate in the stars together? Slivers of disco light hit my arm and I think about how parenting is a fruitless exercise in taming wildness out of our children while we find our weathered skin cracking, revealing the wolves within.

A Tender Place

PROXIMITY TO OTHER FAILED INSTITUTIONS gave Jed a familiar satisfaction now that his marriage was over, so he ignored the faded No Trespassing signs into Detroit's abandoned schools. He'd only seen a few stray dogs and squirrels, no zombie ghost children or living people, yet he felt badass snapping shots of the dilapidation. Jed posted the images to his blog, well trafficked by stay-at-home mothers eager to tsk-tsk the pictorial metaphor of the current state of American education.

Jed was pleased with this artistic social commentary as a healthy, superior alternative to the pathetic gestures he had made in the months after he and Sarah separated. Desperate for connection at the time, he carried flower bouquets everywhere, cheap geraniums or chrysanthemums, and found people passing on the streets responded by projecting their stories onto him—men winked knowingly and women blushed hopefully. When people asked Jed about the occasion, he talked about a friend at rehab, his grandmother at The Home, or his very lucky lady. All lies. On days Jed particularly sought a metaphor for all he had lost, he wore a black patch over his left eye. He told those brave enough to inquire a man named Red had gouged it out with a fork, a jealous lover had doused him with acid, or he had been born without it.

During their marriage, Jed and Sarah made a pact to keep the contents of their bedside tables private. Neither opened the other's drawers and for years this agreement was sufficient until one day, to him, it simply wasn't. While Sarah was out walking the dog, Jed hooked a finger around the brass handle of her top drawer and tugged. Inside was everything he had ever wanted from her.

He flipped through a stack of withheld nightly kisses. Moist and perky, some promised sex, while others were chalky and chaste. A mahogany box, smooth in his palm, emitted a smoky moan when he opened the latch—morning lovemaking locked up tight. Beneath a backpacking trip to Montana and a fat envelope of weekend football games, he discovered a tray of dull compliments about haircuts and biceps. None of it was revolutionary. Mostly Sarah kept kindness in the drawer, and the yeasty, bready smell of it made Jed weep as he realized its lack for so long. Sarah's silence when he admitted the privacy breach and her disinterest in exploring his drawers terrified and embarrassed Jed. He dumped the contents into a shoebox.

As divorce became inevitable, Jed decided if his wife did not want to see the knotted compliments about her staying so fit, or listen to his thousands of prayers for a baby girl, no one would. One day he took the box with him and wandered the grand, century-old hallways of a high school. With the weight of his camera pulling on his neck, he searched for the perfect drawer or supply cabinet in which to hide the box. In one room, an oak sapling pushed through a hill of geometry textbooks and ceiling tiles, its nubile leaves reaching for the brightest squares of light through broken windows. Jed dug through the slipperiness and placed his box deep among the detritus, wondering if the best parts of his marriage would nourish or weaken the tree. He snapped a photo and decided he wouldn't come back to look. Instead, he would post the picture to his blog where all the bored mothers would forever coo over the image's symbolism and praise his artistic eye.

Predator Swamping

BENEATH THE STORE'S FLAT LIGHTING, Audrey could barely discern the pearls' variegated shades of blue, but she knew them by heart. Twisting her arm, the bracelet slid along the tendons, caught on the protruding wrist bone, and complemented her green veins. The fifteen freshwater pearls were irregular in shape and hue. The fourth from the gold clasp was silvery, the seventh held a touch of pink, and the thread hole bruised the twelfth. The lumpy imperfections of the pearls were their strength and their uniqueness made them impenetrable.

One of the children ahead in the checkout line wailed as her mother removed stolen candy from her fist. Audrey counted five children in the brood as her bracelet clattered against the shopping cart's plastic handle, which she realized she had not had wiped clean upon entering the store. One of the five, the only with red hair, slid his nose down into the wet neck-hole of his t-shirt and squeezed his ears. The mother's shirt proclaimed "Espresso then Prosecco." Standing between two carts, one holding the shoplifting toddler and a sleeping baby, the other loaded with cereal and juice boxes and devoid of alcohol, the woman methodically threw items onto the belt, trying to keep up with the teenaged cashier. Instead of gathering the accumulating plastic sacks as requested, children four and five crawled on the floor looking for nickels to use in a nearby stationary horse ride. Audrey could not reach to help.

The pearl bracelet was part of her great grandmother Elsa's set. Audrey's two sisters kept the earrings and choker, and because they never agreed, it was unlikely any of them would wear all three pieces together. Elsa boldly wore all the pearls during weekend solo drives in her early 1900s model electric car. The vehicle required no crank to turn, no muscle, and no sweat on her brow as operating diesel engines did. The seat swiveled out from the cab so Elsa could step onto the sideboard without exposing her ankles—the sight of the delicate knob might unravel unsuspecting men. A woman leaving behind her husband and seven children for a Sunday afternoon would certainly unpin her hair to feel it whip around her neck. Audrey imagined her grandmother leaning out the window, lusting for the forest beyond the road.

Scanning the riot of made-up faces smiling from the magazine stand, Audrey touched each of her fifteen pearls until she reached the clasp, and then reversed direction and counted backwards. She had forgotten black eyeliner for her son, who kept using hers for his band practice. Germs did not concern sixteen-year-olds. No time to return to the cosmetics aisle now; he would be waiting for her to collect him from math tutoring. The trade was stage makeup for a higher SAT score. Audrey told herself bearing only one child held its benefits. There was time and money for negotiating.

She rested on a travel magazine's tropical beach image and shifted her weight, her arches cramping. The cashier called the manager because she couldn't scan the coupon codes, and the candy thief reached out for gum. Audrey clicked her tongue. Through her punch-stained lips, the little girl gave a firm no and snatched peppermint. Audrey did not want more children, no longer cared about little girls and tiny painted fingernails and patent leather shoes with bows, or lip- glosses smelling like lemonade.

When her son had turned thirteen, Audrey's meager family visited Costa Rica and from a distance, watched sea turtles return to the beach of their birth to lay three clutches of eggs. One hundred per clutch, one million nests in all. It rained and the humid air glistened on the bubbly sand. Audrey's son asked the guide why there had to be so many and her husband interrupted to say, "Nature factors in the losses." That evening, after three or four glasses of Guarapo, Audrey cried about running out of time.

The toddler unbuckled herself from the high seat of the cart to reach the bubble gum while her red headed brother counted batteries. Audrey deftly slid along the side of her cart and steadied the child, catching Elsa's bracelet on the candy rack. The fifteen pearls tinkled to the floor and rolled just out of reach in every direction. At Audrey's cry, the mother commanded her children to search beneath the carts and counters. The largest boy held up a pearl like a trophy before his brother took it and tried to shove it into the mechanical horse's coin slot. While everyone was on hands and knees, Audrey clutched the toddler to her hip, threw her purse over her shoulder, and backed out of checkout lane number eight.

Old Growth Forests

HENRY COULD NOT FIND a functioning controller to make the two of them operate the way they used to. Shops did not carry older models. Installing replacement parts failed spectacularly and did nothing to repair the testy conversations about films, burned meals, and arguments over turn-signal use in heavy traffic.

Now Ellen said things like, "What is for dinner is whatever you make us. I am no longer in charge of food." And, "My wedding ring needs cleaning but I can't be bothered."

The broken controller cord habitually tripped them but when they fell together, there was no sex. Henry still yearned for her voice in the dark. He took his hunger with him everywhere, a soft loaf tucked under his arm.

He thought, "I don't know about this love anymore." And, "I hate your taste."

Ellen decorated the walls of their bedroom with paintings and photographs of trees to make up for their barren landscape. Years ago, they had carefully planted trees which might survive the desert climate. All of the firs and even the succulents succumbed. What folly. Henry lay in bed and fantasized about a tree outside the window he could climb and make a nest. The desire gnawed at his insides like a chipmunk.

Ellen threw her hands up and told him controllers were hard to find at this later stage of life, so Henry chewed his nails, reminded himself of his general luck. For instance, he knew from experience lovemaking on dark wood floors creates an especially pretty tableau, and the underside of Ellen's blonde hair was where the curls were tightest. The sublime was always in working order—he could revel in the violet bloom of sunrise, the sound of the front door creaking in the warmth of the afternoon sun.

XOXO

AT 3 A.M., WHEN I MISS PETE most terribly, my heart becomes a baby mouse and squeezes between my ribs until it burrows into my stomach, where it runs the walls until dawn. The floodlights shining on the 12 by 40 billboard pester me while I wait for the mouse to sleep. Pete insisted on the sign because we needed the extra money, and now it's there, and he's gone. The towering, gargantuan, presence in the cornfield next to the farmhouse is a blight on the property. If I turn the lights off someone might miss the management company's phone numbers indicating the sign is available. For a good time, call...

While the firebugs sizzle in the night and the mouse climbs down inside me, I dream of going up and pasting <HEART VACANCY> over the numbers.

The installation wrecks the bucolic scene of our modest property. It interrupts the charming view of our yellow, dilapidated, hundred-year old house snuggled in a grove of Ash and Gum, soft hills in the distance, but I can't take it down now. I have less money than before. A neighboring farm manages the corn and soy rotation for me because I can't muster the energy, but my garden, backside of the house, produces a wealth of tomatoes and squash. I do manage to set up a Farmer's Market stand in town.

Our last paid advertisement on the billboard was for a generic health cereal I never saw in the store. The fussy green and purple script floated over a close-up of what looked suspiciously like crushed pinecones. You can't bark at people about being healthy. It never works. No matter how much fresh produce I offered him *grown on his own damn farm*, Pete subsisted on ham sandwiches on white bread with a side of Marlboros. He's been dead two years now. After he died of a heart attack working in the barn, the image of that fibrous cereal image peeled from the sign all on its own.

"Every farmhouse should have a defibrillator," muttered the EMT when he dutifully tried to revive Pete.

I didn't think that was very helpful. But I did appreciate the sign management company finally sending their crew to strip away the mess.

They covered up the stubborn parts with clean paper and the phone number. A hard reset. No one has called.

Way up along I-65 a billboard screams JESUS IS REAL as you drive north to Illinois. The HELL IS REAL message is equally as loud on the backside when you head south. I don't think a farmer is making any money on that. There's an adult store warehouse an exit or two away from there, and I wonder which came first: the smut or the sign.

Never trust what you read on signs. I could put one up that says <XOXO: WE ARE FRAGILE IN A TERRIBLE WORLD> even though I know that if you're still here, you're strong as thistle.

Before he died, Pete argued with me about going digital. "Relentless messaging is where the real money is."

I told him no. "Too distracting to drivers." I also didn't like the idea of a bordello of light flashing into our bedroom. That's not worth $500. Pete died before he could win that argument.

I think about our bedroom, how unused it feels. Men at the Farmer's Market make me uncomfortable and confuse me. I don't understand their signals or if anyone is ever sending me any. Recently I've been pushing the boundaries of size, experimenting with white chocolate chips and pretzels, beer and avocado dip. Chips, too. It's no kind of marketing plan for a fruit and vegetable peddler to be so doughy, to have fingertips marked with fake orange cheese dust. It began as an unconscious return to the asexuality of my teenage years—binge-watching terrible shows on television with my hand deep in a jellybean jar. Now it's a middle finger to middle age, to all the magazine instructions about what's enjoyable. Have a meaningful relationship! Get the best sex of your life!

I take the advice about getting exercise and swim at the community pool in the mornings.

The first thing I do is take a deep breath, submerge myself, and push off the wall to kick furiously until I reach the other side. Halfway there, my lungs compress, the heart-mouse flattens itself, and I taste agony. I tell myself, *I am more than this.*

Each Saturday I force myself to set up the market tent, to price-mark the crate overflowing with green beans and squash. Young couples scrutinize the tomatoes; weigh them in their palms like small worlds to which they might assign value, as if they are buying a future. I want to shake them by the shoulders: *You can't imagine what's to come.* The girls want bundles of sunflowers, and I tie stalks with little ribbons, make them pretty, then I add the ends of the grosgrain to the tip of my graying braid, talismans against certain decrepitude, for all of us.

Foot Licking Bandit

I licked my first foot at the neighborhood supermarket. It belonged to a slim girl of eighteen whose white sandals revealed toes meticulously painted an appetizing tangerine. Craving orange juice, I turned away in search of refreshment, but she followed me down the aisle. Prior to this occasion, I was less the fetish type and more a woman struggling with turning thirty.

In search of wisdom, I sought the advice of others nearing the same milestone. They were naively hopeful and assumed my union was a measure of comfort. "Not that being married ensures happiness, but it helps."

Women in their forties and fifties were devastatingly bitter. "When you turn thirty-one you'll see that no one pays any attention at all."

"Oh, honey," said women beyond sixty. "You're a baby."

On that Tuesday at Shaw's, as the teenage girl clip-clopped across the linoleum, her plump toes entranced me. I don't know why. She perused yogurts and I found myself kneeling beside her.

I politely asked, "May I try a sample?"

Her doe eyes flashed quizzically and I lunged at her calf, cradled her sandal, and made a wild, determined lick with my tongue across all the toes of her right foot.

She squealed, pushed against my crouched torso, and jerked her leg away. Ears buzzing, I stumbled. Salt, dirt, and paint mingled in my mouth. The sensation of my tongue sliding into the valleys of her warm flesh—it was all more than I could bear. I was immediately addicted to the transgression.

I have since licked hundreds of feet and with each taste, I absorb the very essence of youth. Have you ever been close to a twenty-three-year-old with gunmetal gray toenails and breathed the fecund, rosy air of her body? When I lick the round innocence of her delicate pinky toe, I too am seven years younger. The world expands before me. I have not settled down with one lover, waiting to become molding parchment. I am not an unsure, blind insect scuttling along corporate ladders. There isn't a growing chasm between my kaleidoscopic childhood and me.

When the Foot-Licking Bandit strikes, she is less a woman entering her fourth decade and more a woman taking time.

Pineapple Pattern Cut-Out Swimsuit, Girl's Size 7

IT WOULD TAKE A FEW HOURS to reach the amusement park where she would hold her two- year-old brother's hands through the splash pad fountains and guide him on the climbers, and he was asleep now next to her in the backseat, hot drool collecting on his chin, so Lila tried to nap too. When she asked her mother how she could make her own tummy flat her mother did not say, "You don't need to do that, honey." She did not say, "Oh, your belly is wonderful." Instead, she told Lila the trick was to suck it in as tight as she could several times a day. "That's what I do." Her mother also taught boot camp classes and ran 5ks and played tennis and ate Greek yogurt and a cucumber for lunch and said she liked it. Lila's father did not like women who looked like cows.

The station wagon's wheezy air conditioning hardly reached the backseat but Lila's mother hated the tornado sound of open windows on the highway. Sweat matted Lila's hairline and the underside of her pale rectangular thighs peeled and sucked at the vinyl upholstery. She pulled in her little roll of belly fat back against her spine, as her mother advised, and attempted the most uncomfortable nap. When Lila opened her eyes, her mother was pulling into the parking lot. Lila was delighted to find her stomach muscles remained miraculously clenched, although a weird nausea accompanied the sensation. The car always smelled like her father's cigarettes.

"I did it, Mom!" Lila reported.

Her mother's mouth was a tight line as she leaned over her brother and clicked open the safety-seat belt. He kicked his chubby thighs. Delicious.

Narcissus and the Beaver

A POWERFUL WILDCAT would gleam in the choking early light, but she squints, instincts atrophied. When she was fourteen the fashion magazines tainted her, told her acceptable legs touch only at the ankles and knees, and even now she remains unable to inhabit herself as a marvelous lioness. The daily runs rarely stray from a paved loop through neighborhoods whose streets bear the names of more interesting places.

A manmade pond squats in the hill she conquers by visualizing helium balloons attached to her kneecaps with invisible strings, making her effort light. Spring's humidity turns her lungs to sponge. The sad body of water does its best impression of nature. Algae crawls the surface in August, cattails sway in the marshy spots each fall, and later, snow drowns itself. This morning a sylph-like insect disrupts the surface before it darts from one beaver mound to the next. Each night the beavers work on their lodges and create outposts, and each morning she notes new construction. Ten piles of stick and mud rise now from the water, tenuous protection from what may stalk the surrounding meadow. At what point will the pond no longer sustain its industrious clan?

How many miles must she run until she is complete? Achieving thigh-gap at her age is a package deal with a sharp jaw and papery skin—there is no glamour in being slender any more. The magazines say she can apply mascara to the bottom lashes because she is losing natural pigmentation and otherwise looks erased. At the highest point on the hill, she pauses to sip from her water bottle and roars across the languid water. It reflects nothing. Tomorrow she could leave the pavement, follow the trail behind the pond into the woods. She will learn to hunt and feed.

There is a splash in the water behind her and the sleek black head of a beaver emerges. It slides elegantly despite its roundness and swims to the nearest mound before diving. She makes a pact with the animal to return so she can ask how the beaver knows when to build, how it determines the height and complexity of the structure, how it knows when it will be finished.

Tests of Agility

WHEN NECESSARY, THE INSTITUTE COMPELLED Tamara to travel to the children's homes to administer tests. She flew on cheap late-night flights to the destination small town or labyrinthine suburb. Past midnight in Kentucky, a hail of June bugs splattered against the windshield. The stipends only covered low-end motels next to truck stops and Tamara checked into a dim, wood- paneled room reminiscent of a horse stable, where she reviewed her testing equipment before passing out on the musty bed.

In the morning, she packed up her rental car and a long-haul trucker sidled up in the parking lot and propositioned her. Tamara invited him to join her for breakfast.

In the diner a young waitress took their order of flapjacks and coffee before eagerly sharing the cause of her recent familial difficulties.

"My mother is very Christian and never wanted me to try yoga because the spiritual part?" her voice swung up, "that's worshipping other gods."

The trucker tilted the brim of his cap and squinted at the girl, ravenous.

Tamara habitually shared information she read in magazines. She wanted to tell the waitress the Church forced unmarried pregnant women to live in special orphanages in medieval times. Nuns immediately separated mothers from their offspring after they gave birth. For an entire year the women remained cloistered while they nursed other babies, never their own.

Undecided whether or not she wanted children, Tamara knew she would never have any.

"But when I tried a yoga class last month, I felt a deep connection to my body." The girl fiddled with a ladybug broach on her collar. "It was transformative."

Tamara let the girl ramble, uneducated.

"I still haven't told my parents about it and maybe this is my rebellion? Anyway. Did you want cream?"

Tamara waved her off and explained to the trucker that she would drive into Paducah to test children whose parents enrolled them in a study as infants. Monitors like Tamara evaluated the children their entire lives. It was lonely, repetitive work. Were they intelligent? Tamara asked questions to determine this. Coordinated? She gave them tests of agility. Some children were separated from their parents at birth and scientists wanted to know the affects.

The trucker scowled and told Tamara about his sons and wife back in some middle place, how he saw them only a few days a month.

Tamara closed her eyes and inhaled. She nestled her hands into the Namaste prayer position between her breasts and looked at the man.

"All you're getting from me is breakfast."

She hoped he was the type of trucker who read the signs on the bathroom walls about child trafficking, that he was the type of man who refused to be serviced by thirteen-year-old runaways, but these were questions she would not ask.

After she cajoled the seven-year-old test subject into hours of tasks, Tamara made her way to the next family in Tennessee. She skipped dinner and pulled off the highway onto a nameless road where no one would know to find her. Leaning against a white fence, she laced up sneakers to run free. While jogging through rolling countryside in the early twilight haze she reached a green barn at the top of a hill on which someone had painted an impressive white cross. A horse emerged, startling Tamara. Its nostrils flared but it leaned over the fence, its head low. It too was alone, and Tamara tentatively reached for its nose, deciding to call it Rooster or Cactus. She settled on Romeo and when she turned around and accelerated back down the hill, she invited him to follow.

"Let's race to the bottom," she told the animal, the rhythm of its hooves in tandem with her pounding sneakers, "And the winner gets to jump the fence."

New Wavelengths

THE SIRENS WENT OFF while Amelia sipped alleged coffee from a paper cone and waited for news of her car's lubrication needs. She picked perfumed grit from her crowded bottom teeth, still bristling from the mechanic's lurid review of her physique.

"Welcome to Pete's Autobody." Emphasis on the second syllable.

The brightening air reinforced Amelia's vote in the last election for chimes to replace the previous rainbow alert system's headache-inducing pulses. How delightful.

The mechanic popped his head into the room and made an announcement before surveying her legs.

"This one's a stunner!"

"Double?"

"Triple!"

Triple rainbow migrations were new to the region and Amelia did not want to miss one. She rushed outside, dirtying her blouse with the cone's grey liquid. The ashy rivulets staining the cream fabric did not matter, nor did she care she would have to stop home to change before work. Amelia would insert a cover slide to her presentation deck with a photo of the Triple and the conference room would fall to a hush while she described the arc trinity.

The iridescent wavelengths produce a euphoric neurological affect, a throbbing joy. The Earth's magnetic core pulls the spiked ends of the rainbow into its dirt, and the rainbow responds in kind with clenched teeth, refusing to dissolve. Time bends. Trapped beneath such a beast means tickling the underside of the closest band and pushing against the forgiving, gelatinous space between the nanometers where color does and does not exist.

Before moving on to her planned charts and graphs, Amelia would explain how a Triple eventually snaps into itself and disappears, and her colleagues would search out the window behind her, as if the intensity of hope could re-form such glory. Amelia would not reveal how she harnessed the power of newly discovered wavelengths to bore holes through the mechanic. She would not bullet-point how she punished him for ranking in his mind the round perkiness of her breasts and the height of her heels, how she carved a sinuous amalgam of color into the chest flap of his baby blue coveralls. The force of action dissipated along with the Triple and Amelia intuited the sirens would have to ring before she could employ it again. She couldn't wait.

Hey Honey, You Can Play My Flute Anytime

In Patelson's Music House, Mari thumbed through the sheet music for flute, her wool coat dripping, her breath irregular from the hurried walk. The Bach concerto for strings playing over the sound system did not soothe her. She knew the man who had followed her from the subway was standing outside the shop. He was a squat, revolting creature.

On the subway, his kinetic, daring stare had disturbed her reading. She had hoped to break his dark spell once she reached the street surface, but even once she rounded Carnegie Hall and paused to look back, he was there, his face shadowed by a cap.

As a child, fairies and foxes had followed her. On lucky days, out of the corner of her eye, she caught sight of the elves hiding in the shadows. Now grown up, Mari mostly encountered trolls and goons who were not afraid to make themselves known and say things aloud. She battled them all too often.

Mari thought to stay inside Patelson's as she snatched the packet for Faure's *Fantaisie*. She nearly told the cashier she needed help protecting herself.

Instead, she tucked the parcel into her bag, exhaled, and opened the door. He was waiting near the curb, stubby and wan. She searched for his eyes, her mouth a fierce, ready weapon, and then she turned away. Today she fled. Back to the subway, back to her errands, troll be gone!

She flew down the subway stairs, back underground, through the turnstile, and onto a waiting train. The doors closed behind her, nearly catching her long hair, but she had outrun him.

The car smelled of sweet rot. A puffy homeless man had half the place to himself and his garbage bag of cans. Mari stood in the space between him and the passengers huddled at the far end of the car. He winked at Mari before he closed his eyes and pretended to surf the wet floor, the train's increasing speed animating him. Only a few minutes passed before the heavy door connecting the cars behind him opened, and the man in the cap appeared. The goon had made the train and was searching for her. He smiled grotesquely.

The train lurched as it pulled into a station and the homeless surfer lost his balance and knocked into the goon. Flustered, the homeless man grabbed his things and jumped on to the platform once the doors opened. His black bag ripped and soda cans clattered everywhere.

Kneeling on the platform, he wailed and frantically scooped at the cans. For a moment Mari was stuck, calculating the opportunity to escape while her goon was distracted. Instead she shifted her mission and yelled at the homeless man to stay where he was as she corralled and kicked cans out to him through the doorway.

When the doors closed, her energy was an undeniable, humming force. Mari turned and began to throw the remaining cans at the man in the cap, aiming for his chest and head, and she hit him over and over again. She picked sticky cans from the muddy floor, where small hands in the shadows rolled them to her. She unleashed her fury, forcing the goon backwards until he retreated to the darkness from which he'd come.

The Luster of Minerals

JADE CONSIDERED ORDERING THE VAGINAL BEADS Gwyn raved about in the absurd hope that ritualistically inserting a smooth stone might resolve her inner conflicts.

"They're not all made of jade, but of course you should buy those." Gwyn proselytized every item her famous namesake's lifestyle website promoted.

"And practicing with them will clear my chi?" Jade did not keep up with the best way to live.

"The beads increase positivity, but I prefer the strengthening benefits. I've been using one for six weeks and my husband loves it." She winked.

Jade adjusted her wide-brimmed hat and squinted at her phone. It was late August and she and Gwyn were keeping minimal track of the children at the neighborhood pool. The website cautioned that beginners should use quartz rather than jade. How advanced were her demons?

"Will it replenish my lost glow?" Jade rolled her eyes as she moved the conversation into infomercial territory.

Gwyn sucked on a vodka-soaked gummi bear and replied in earnest. "Of course, darling. All good things."

Jade stirred her drink and pondered. Perhaps her friend's luster had intensified over the last few weeks but she honestly couldn't say, since Gwyn also paid for weekly pore-minimizing facials and juiced most of her calories. Gwyn had confessed the dentist was shooting her forehead wrinkles with paralyzing fillers. The woman could not have been more luminous were she a toddler who regularly exfoliated naked with fine Tahitian sands during family vacations.

Gwyn's confident war on aging had a twisted appeal, but the fresh vanity accompanying middle age was the very animus Jade sought to conquer. She panicked every time she plucked a chin hair or flopped her slack breasts into a bra, but the desire to battle both time and nature was what she wanted to destroy. Jade sometimes slashed purple lipstick beneath her eyes and filled in her forehead lines with black eyeliner. It was all war paint that never saw the outside of the bathroom.

Now was the time to turn to the substance of the beauty myth. Now was the time to celebrate, not erase, the accumulated evidence of life. For decades, Jade starved and exercised herself to attract a partner, and once he had given her babies, they kneaded her body into a soft dough. To hell with the time she was expected to spend in Pilates classes to reduce belly squish and the high price of European smoothing creams.

"This is when it counts," she said aloud.

"Sweetheart, look after yourself, because no one else will." The afternoon blurred around the edges.

A woman Jade had seen around town placed her bag on a nearby chaise lounge and casually peeled off her shirt to reveal a bare chest. No bikini. No breasts. An artful tattoo of roses and vines covered her torso. Dusky red petals and muted gray-green leaves climbed her ribcage.

The woman smiled radiantly, strode past in black boy shorts, and dove into the pool, scattering their daughters. Jade nodded with approval and wonder. The tattoos weren't meant to camouflage a missing part or make do with new circumstances. They reclaimed beauty outside of the approval of men.

"Well, that's certainly a choice," Gwyn said disconcertedly.

Jade loved Gwyn dearly and wanted to hug her tanned, bony shoulders, but the space between them had now grown too great. She couldn't reach her. Jade hoped the tattooed woman walked around all summer without a shirt on—to the farmer's market and the ball fields, to the gym.

Jade took off her hat and stretched up to the sky. She began to plan a gathering for women interested in underscoring the years of their lives with decorative enhancements. The jokey online photo she had recently seen of a woman with tiny sequins pasted on her under-eye circles was ingenious. She imagined peacock feathered-crowns atop gray or thinning hair.

Iridescent body paint lovingly swirled around cellulite and silver rivers mapping stretch marks. Jade beads for inner strength. She slipped into the pool and approached the woman with the tattoos. She would ask her to be a general in a new army of intentional, commanding female bodies, marching unabashedly and artfully in time.

Acknowledgements

The author wishes to express much gratitude to the editors of the following publications, wherein the stories below appeared as earlier versions:

"Things to Do While Listening to Your Brother on the Phone" and "Radioactive" appeared in *Whiskey Paper*; "National Treasure" appeared in *People Holding*; "The Girl and the Fox Pirate" appeared published in *Pithead Chapel*; "Fat Girl Lament" and "I See the Way Your Eyes Follow Me at Target" appeared in *Literary Orphans*; "Give Me Your Hand and I Will Pull You Up" appeared in *Chicago Literati*; "Ruby Throated" appeared in the *Atticus Review*; "Flight Helmet" appeared in *Cheap Pop*; "Underwater" appeared in *Halo Literary Magazine*; "The Motherhood Gig" appeared in *Luna Luna Magazine*; "A Tender Place" appeared in *Midwestern Gothic*; "XOXO" appeared in *Third Point Press*; "The Foot-Licking Bandit" appeared in *971 Menu*.

Photo by Susan Fletcher Conaway

Kate Gehan was born and raised in New York City and is a graduate of Haverford College and Emerson College's MFA program. Among many publications, her writing has appeared in *McSweeney's Internet Tendency, Split Lip Magazine, Literary Mama, People Holding,* and as a winner of *Midwestern Gothic*'s Flash Fiction Summer 2016 series. Kate read as a cast member of the 2014 Listen to Your Mother show and her work has been nominated for the Pushcart Prize, The Best of the Net, and Wigleaf's Top 50 (Very) Short Fictions. She lives with her family in the Midwest.

Enjoy more Mojave River Press titles

EVERY KISS A WAR – Stories by Leesa Cross-Smith
Available at MojaveRiverPress.com (under Buy Books) and as an ebook from all major ebook retailers

"Leesa Cross-Smith is a consummate storyteller who uses her formidable talents to tell the oft-overlooked stories of people living in that great swath of place between the left and right coasts. She offers thrilling turns of phrases, but where she is most stunning is in the endings of each of the 27 stories, creating crisp, evocative moments that will linger long after you've read this book's very last word."
—ROXANE GAY, author of *An Untamed State*

ROADSIDE EPIPHANIES – Poems by Michael Dwayne Smith
Available at MojaveRiverPress.com (under Buy Books)

"From an unswerving devotion to poetry, Michael Dwayne Smith's images amplify outward from the Mojave Desert to the sordid metropolis of Los Angeles, and on up into California's northern regions. But Roadside Epiphanies is far from parochial. With clarity and keen control of sentiment, Smith is mindful of the need to express poignant truth in the simple, yet pungent smell of cigarettes in a young girl's tangled hair, or in "any space / alive with emptiness." He renders to us the world at large—the universe in a cholla needle, something of Blake's world in a grain of sand. There is much to admire in the depth and breadth of Smith's lines. His striking and eloquent control of language and image make this collection of poems a delight to behold."
—JEFFREY ALFIER, author of *Fugue for a Desert Mountain*, winner of the Kithara Book Prize